OTHER YEARLING BOOKS YOU WILL ENJOY:

YEARLING BOOKS are designed especially to entertain and enlighten young people. Charles F. Reasoner, Professor Emeritus of Children's Literature and Reading, New York University, is consultant to this series.

For a complete listing of all Yearling titles, write to:
Dell Publishing Co., Inc., Promotion Department,
P.O. Box 3000, Pine Brook, N.J. 07058.

CAM JANSEN

and the
Mystery of the
Monster Movie

★ ★

DAVID A. ADLER
Illustrated by Susanna Natti

★ ★

A YEARLING BOOK

Published by
Dell Publishing Co., Inc.
1 Dag Hammarskjold Plaza
New York, New York 10017

Yearling ® TM 913705, Dell Publishing Co., Inc.

ISBN: 0-440-41022-3

Reprinted by arrangement with The Viking Press.

Printed in the United States of America

July 1986

10 9 8 7 6 5 4 3 2 1

CW

To Sally Cipriano

Chapter One

It was a cold winter Sunday afternoon. Cam Jansen and her friend Eric Shelton were waiting in line outside a movie theater. Cam's parents were with them.

Cam's eyes were closed.

"What's the big headline on top of the movie posters?" Eric asked.

"That's easy," Cam said. " 'Monster Movie Month Continues. Now Showing—' "

"And what's printed on the first poster?" Eric asked.

"Let's see," Cam said with her eyes still

closed. "There's a parade of giant brown, white, and black shoes. '*Shoe Escape*,' it says. 'Starring Joe Roberts, Angela Kane, and Robert Allen.'

"I can tell you what's on the other poster,

too," Cam said. "And I can tell you what you're wearing and that one of your shoelaces is untied."

Eric tied his shoelace as Cam opened her eyes. Cam has what people call a photographic memory. They mean that Cam's mind takes a picture of whatever she sees. When Cam wants to remember something, even a detail like a name on a movie poster, she just looks at the picture stored in her brain.

"Do you know the last time I saw *Shoe Escape*?" Cam's father asked. "It was one week before our wedding. It was really something."

"Yes," Cam's mother said. "I wore a beautiful white gown. My hair was set in curls."

"At the beginning of the movie," Cam's father said, "everything is quiet. Children just like you and Eric are going to school. Ordinary people, like your mother and me, are going to work. And they're all wearing shoes."

"I wore white shoes at our wedding," Cam's mother said.

"You know," Cam's father went on, "sometimes I see just ordinary people, like that woman with the red hat or that man over there with the cane, and I think that I saw them in *Shoe Escape*. That's what's so great about this movie. It's about ordinary people and ordinary shoes."

A light snow began to fall. Cam's mother told Cam and Eric to close the top buttons on their coats.

"Cam, take a good look at me," Eric said as he buttoned his coat. "I want to test your memory again. This time I bet I'll stump you."

"Cam remembers everything," her mother said.

Cam took a few steps back and looked straight at Eric. She said, *"Click,"* and closed

4

her eyes. Cam always says *"Click"* when she wants to remember something. She says it's the sound her mental camera makes when it takes a picture.

Cam's real name is Jennifer Jansen. When she was younger, people called her "Red" because she has red hair. But when they found out about her amazing photographic memory, they began calling her "The Camera." Soon "The Camera" was shortened to "Cam."

"This time I tricked you," Eric said. "I asked you to take a good look at me. If you did, you should have seen the posters right behind me, too."

"I did."

"How many spider legs are there on the second poster?"

The line started to move. But Cam just stood there. Her eyes were still closed.

"What are you doing?" Eric asked.

"I'm counting legs. There are five spiders on the poster and each has eight legs. That's forty legs." Cam opened her eyes. "Am I right?"

"Yes," Eric said. "Now come on. Your parents are way ahead of us."

Cam and Eric caught up with Cam's parents at the ticket window.

"Two adults and two children," Mrs. Jansen said. Then she passed some money through the window.

"How old are the children?" the ticket seller asked.

"They're both ten."

The ticket seller gave Cam's mother two purple tickets, two green tickets, and some change. Then Cam, Eric, and Cam's parents went into the theater.

The lobby was crowded and warm. A few people were standing and talking. Others were waiting in line to buy popcorn and soda.

"We can get food later," Cam's father

said. "I want to get good seats. And I don't want to miss anything."

They went through the swinging doors and into the theater. Soft music was playing. People were sitting in many of the seats. Cam's father found four empty seats near the front of the theater. Cam and Eric took off their coats and sat down. Then they looked up at the dark, blank screen and waited.

Chapter Two

Cam's father turned and looked at the balcony and at the rest of the theater. "Look how crowded it is here!" he said. "And I'll bet lots of these people saw *Shoe Escape* when it first came out. They want to see it again, just as I do."

Cam tapped her mother on her shoulder and asked, "Can Eric and I get some popcorn?"

Mrs. Jansen gave Cam some money and said, "Get two buckets. One for you and Eric, and one for your father and me."

"I wonder why *Shoe Escape* has never been shown on TV," Cam's father said as Cam and Eric squeezed past him.

As Cam and Eric walked down the aisle toward the swinging doors, Mr. Jansen called to them, "Hurry back."

The lobby was still crowded. There were a few people waiting to buy popcorn, candy, ice cream, and soda.

"I'll wait in line," Eric said. "I want to test your memory again. Look at me, the way you did the last time."

Cam stood back and looked at Eric. She was also careful to look at the other people in line. There was a short, heavy man with a gray beard. After him there were a woman with a large red hat, two older boys, a woman in a pink running suit, and Eric. Cam looked at them all. She closed her eyes and said, *"Click."* Then Cam opened her eyes and looked at the price list and at the woman behind the counter. Cam closed her

eyes again and said, *"Click."* She was walk-
ing toward Eric with her eyes still closed
when she heard someone shouting.

"I paid for a full bucket of popcorn! This
one is half empty!"

Cam opened her eyes. It was the man
with the gray beard who was shouting. He
was showing the people in line his bucket
and asking them, "Does this look full? Does
this look full?"

Eric whispered to Cam, "That bucket is
almost full. I don't know why he's making
such a fuss."

The theater manager came out. He asked
the woman behind the counter what the
problem was. She pointed to the man with
the beard.

"Oh, it's you, Mr. Bender," the manager
said. "Look, I don't go to your theater to
make trouble. I wish you wouldn't come
here."

"Well, in my theater," Mr. Bender said to

the people in line, "our popcorn buckets are filled to the top. And people coming to Bender's Bargain Theater get to see a triple feature—three great movies for the price of one."

The theater manager took the bucket from Mr. Bender. He gave it to the woman behind the counter. "Please pour some more in for Mr. Bender," he said.

The woman poured a huge scoop of popcorn into the bucket. When Mr. Bender walked away with it, popcorn spilled. He left a trail of popcorn from the counter to the doors of the theater.

The next woman in line wanted change for the telephone. The boys bought soda and popcorn. The woman in the running suit bought two ice cream cones. Then Cam and Eric bought two medium-size buckets of popcorn. They were filled to the very top.

Just as Cam and Eric opened the doors

to the theater, the lights dimmed. The movie was about to begin.

Cam and Eric rushed to their seats. As they sat down, soft marching music started to play. The music became louder, and the screen lit up with a picture of a marching band. At first the screen showed the marchers' faces. Then it showed their feet and their shoes. Then two words seemed to shoot out onto the screen: *"Shoe Escape."*

There were pictures of the movie's stars: Joe Roberts, Angela Kane, and Robert Allen. After their faces and names were shown on the screen, their shoes were shown.

"I think I've seen that woman somewhere," Cam whispered to Eric when Angela Kane was shown.

"Well, I don't think she's the real star of this movie. I think her shoes are," Eric said.

Cam took a handful of popcorn and looked up at the screen. It was early in the morning. A man was just finishing getting dressed. He was tying his shoes. When the man ate his breakfast, one of the threads holding his shoe together broke. Another thread broke. As the man walked along a busy street on the way to work, threads on both shoes opened up. His shoes were coming apart.

The man stopped and waited at a corner. Other people stopped, too. The threads on their shoes were opening up.

Without looking away from the screen, Cam quickly ate the popcorn in her hand. As she took another handful, Eric whispered, "This is scary."

"It's only a movie," Cam told him. "It could never happen."

The man was standing in an elevator. Other people in the elevator were talking to him, wishing him a good morning. Then the screen showed their shoes. The threads on the other shoes were breaking, too.

The man got off on the eighth floor of
the building. But the doors to the elevator
didn't close. The man sat down at his desk.
He felt something move beneath him. It
was his shoes. They walked off his feet and
ran out the office door. In the hall other
shoes were running. They all ran into the

elevator. The doors closed. At the seventh floor the doors opened and more men's and women's shoes ran in. Then the screen became dark.

"What happened?" Cam asked.

"It's the shoes," her father said. "They're all getting together. The movie gets real exciting now."

"I don't mean about the shoes. Why did the movie stop?"

Chapter Three

"While we wait," Eric said to Cam, "let's finish that memory test."

Cam closed her eyes. She said, *"Click."*

"What color shoes was the woman just ahead of me in line wearing?"

"You're trying to trick me again, Eric. She wasn't wearing shoes. She was wearing a pink running suit and white sneakers."

"What color eyeglasses was Mr. Bender wearing?"

"He wasn't wearing eyeglasses."

"What color were his shoes?"

"Brown."

"That's right," Eric said.

Cam opened her eyes. People around her were talking. Some wanted to know why the movie had stopped. Others wondered what the shoes did next.

"I think the shoes all go dancing," a man behind Cam said.

"No. Shoes don't like to dance. They all go to a shoeshine stand."

"I think they run to the park and play football."

Cam's father shook his head. Then he turned around and said, "None of you is right. But I won't tell you what happens. That would ruin the fun."

"Dad," Cam said, "can I get some soda? All that popcorn made me thirsty."

Mr. Jansen gave Cam some money. She and Eric squeezed past Cam's parents. They were just about to walk into the lobby when the theater manager walked in.

18

"Let's wait and hear what he says," Cam told Eric.

The theater manager walked onto the stage. He buttoned his jacket, straightened his tie, and waited. A few people in the theater saw him standing there. They stopped talking. Then others saw him. Soon the theater was quiet.

"We seem to be having some trouble with our film *Shoe Escape*. I am sorry for the delay, but I do promise that the film will begin again shortly."

The theater manager started to walk off the stage. Then he stopped, smiled, and said, "And I can tell you, this movie will be worth the wait."

"Come on," Cam said to Eric. "Let's get our soda before the movie starts again."

Cam and Eric rushed into the lobby. The theater manager was right behind them. There was a line of people waiting to buy refreshments. Cam and Eric stood at the end of the line. The theater manager walked past them and up a dark, narrow staircase in the corner of the lobby.

"We're next," Eric said.

"Can I help you?" the woman behind the counter asked.

"We'd like two small cups of soda, please," Cam said. "I want cola."

"And I want orange," Eric told the woman.

The woman took two cups from a large stack of cups on her side of the counter.

She filled each with soda and held them out to Cam and Eric. Cam put the money on the counter and reached for the soda. Just then they heard some yelling.

"It's from up there," Cam said. She pointed to the narrow staircase.

Cam ran to the staircase. Eric followed her.

"But what about your soda?" the woman behind the counter called out.

"They're arguing about something up there," Cam told Eric. "But I don't know what they're saying. Come on. Let's go up there and listen."

"Maybe it's none of our business," Eric said.

But Cam was already halfway up the stairs. Eric followed her.

The staircase led to a narrow door. The small plastic sign on the door said: PROJECTION ROOM. KEEP OUT. The door was partly open.

"How could you let something like this happen?" one man said. It sounded to Cam and Eric like the theater manager.

"I didn't let anything happen," another man said. "I showed the first reel, just as I always do. But when I looked for the second reel, it was gone."

"Look at this mess. I've asked you to clean

it up. It's probably buried under all these coffee cups and newspapers."

"It's not buried anywhere. I put it right here on the table. I didn't lose it. Someone took it."

"Did you hear that?" Eric whispered. "Someone stole a reel of film."

"Sh."

"It's your job to make sure that there's a movie showing on that screen," the theater manager said.

"I know," the other man answered. "I was here just about the whole time."

"Start showing the second movie. Then we'll both see if we can find the missing film."

"Come on, Cam," Eric said. "He's coming out."

Chapter Four

Cam and Eric raced down the steps. Just as they reached the lobby, the theater manager started down the steps.

"Oh, there you are," the woman behind the counter said to Cam and Eric. "Take these sodas before they spill."

Cam and Eric took the two cups of soda. Then they followed the theater manager into the theater.

"What took you so long?" Cam's father asked when Cam and Eric came to their seats.

24

"Sh," Cam's mother said. She pointed to the theater manager. He was standing on the stage.

"I must tell you again that I'm sorry," the theater manager said. "We have a problem with our first feature. While we try to work on that, we hope you'll enjoy watching our second feature, *The Monster Spiders.* It will begin in just a few minutes."

Cam whispered to her mother, "The second reel of *Shoe Escape* is gone. Someone stole it."

Cam turned and watched the theater manager as he walked past. The lights dimmed. Music started to play.

"Look," Cam said. "He stopped at Mr. Bender's seat."

"Sh. The movie is starting," Cam's father said.

"They're arguing."

Cam's mother and Eric turned. Cam's father didn't.

"They're both leaving the theater. I'm going to see what's happening," Cam said.

"You're not going out there alone," Cam's mother whispered. "I'm going with you."

"Me, too," Eric said.

Cam's father didn't seem to notice when Cam, Eric, and Mrs. Jansen left their seats. On the movie screen a scientist was coating

a bug with liquid vitamins. Then he fed the bug to a spider. Mr. Jansen's eyes didn't leave the screen.

As soon as Cam opened the door to the lobby, she heard the men arguing. "Bring back that reel of film or I'll call the police," the theater manager said.

"I don't have your film."

"First you come in here and make a fuss about the popcorn. Then you steal the film. I'm having you arrested."

"Don't sell half-empty buckets of popcorn and I won't complain."

The two men were standing very close to each other. The theater manager walked a few steps back. "I need that film now," he said. "I have a whole theater filled with people waiting to see it. If you give it to me now, I'll forget about calling the police."

The theater manager and Mr. Bender were standing in the middle of the lobby. Cam, Eric, and Cam's mother were standing in a corner near the doors to the theater. The two men didn't seem to notice them.

"Do you think he took it?" Eric whispered.

"I think so," Cam's mother said. "He has a motive. A motive is like a reason. Mr. Bender's reason for taking the film is so that people won't want to come to this theater anymore. Then they'll go to his instead. That's why he complained about the popcorn."

"It won't help you to keep that film," the theater manager said. "The newspapers will report what you did. That kind of publicity could ruin a theater like yours."

Cam closed her eyes and said, *"Click."*

"What are you doing?" Cam's mother asked.

"I'm looking at Mr. Bender. I'm trying to remember when I first saw him. Maybe he had the film hidden under his coat."

Cam said, "*Click,*" again.

"Now what are you looking at?" Eric asked.

"I'm looking at all the other people I saw in the lobby. Maybe I saw someone else who had the film hidden."

"Well," the theater manager said to Mr. Bender. "Are you going to give me that film or not?"

"I don't have that film," Mr. Bender said. "I didn't take it."

"Then I'm calling the police. You just make sure that you don't leave the theater before they get here."

Chapter Five

The theater manager walked into his office. Mr. Bender looked at a few of the movie posters in the lobby. Then he went into the men's room.

"I'll bet that's where he hid the film," Eric said. "I'll bet it's at the bottom of the wastebasket under the paper towels. As soon as he leaves, I'll go in and find it."

Cam's eyes were still closed. "I looked at the pictures I have in my head of the people I saw in the lobby. I didn't see anyone holding a reel of film." Cam opened her eyes. "But I did see something strange. And I remembered something."

"What was it? What did you remember?" Cam's mother asked.

"The man in the projection room said, 'I was here *just about* the whole time.' That means that he wasn't there the whole time. He must have left the projection room. Now what would get him to leave his job?"

"Maybe he had to go to the men's room," Eric said. "Maybe Mr. Bender was waiting for him there."

"Or maybe," Cam said, "there was a telephone call for him."

"Yes," Cam's mother said. "A telephone call would get him away from his job."

Cam started to climb the narrow steps to the projection room. "Come on," she told her mother and Eric. "Let's find out."

Cam's mother and Eric followed Cam. They knocked on the door of the projection room.

"It's not locked. Come on in," a man's voice called from inside.

Cam pushed the door open. A man was sitting on a metal folding chair behind a large movie projector. All around the man's chair were coffee cups and old newspapers.

"Can I help you?" the man asked. Then he saw Cam's mother looking at the mess on the floor. "I was just about to clean up," he said.

"I know that someone stole the second reel of *Shoe Escape*," Cam said. "I think it happened when you left this room."

"How do you know I left the room?"

"You spoke to someone on the telephone."

"No, I didn't."

"You didn't," Cam said. She looked down at the floor and gently kicked one of the empty cups. "I thought I had this all figured out."

"I was called to the telephone. Someone had an 'important message' for me. But when I got there, no one was on the other end."

"That's it!" Cam said. "I know who called you, and I know who took the film."

Cam ran out of the room and started down the steps to the lobby. Eric was about to follow her.

"That's my daughter, Jennifer," Cam's mother told the man in the projection room. "She has an amazing memory. If she says she knows who took the film, I'm sure she does."

"Come on, Mrs. Jansen," Eric said. "We have to hurry and catch Cam."

Once they were down the stairs, Mrs. Jansen looked across the lobby. Eric ran past the woman who collected the tickets, to the front doors of the theater. He looked outside. The snow was falling heavily now. It had covered the sidewalk. Eric saw some-one shoveling the walk in front of the the-ater. A young couple had stopped to read the movie posters. But Eric didn't see Cam.

Eric closed the door. "I can't find her," he told Cam's mother. "Maybe she went back into the theater."

Then Mrs. Jansen walked past a small open room. She stopped and said, "There she is."

Cam was standing between two public telephones. She was looking through one

of the telephone books. Cam pointed to a
name on one page and said, "I found her.
She lives at 358 Taft Drive."

"Who lives on Taft Drive?" Eric asked.

"Angela Kane," Cam said as she walked
toward the front doors of the theater.

"Jennifer Jansen, where are you going?"
her mother asked.

"To get back the missing film."

"You're not going out there without a coat. And you're not going anywhere until you explain to me what's going on."

"But, Mom," Cam said, "I'm sure I know who stole *Shoe Escape*, and we have to hurry to get the movie back before the end of *The Monster Spiders*."

"Well," Cam's mother said, "if you say you know who stole the film, I believe you. You're good at figuring these things out. I'll get the coats. Then I'll drive you. But you have to promise to explain everything to me in the car."

"I promise."

Cam's mother went back into the theater to get the coats. While Cam and Eric waited for her, two police officers walked in. "They're going to arrest Mr. Bender," Cam whispered, "and he didn't take the film. I'm sure of it."

Chapter Six

Cam's mother came out of the theater and gave Cam and Eric their coats. Mrs. Jansen waited while they put on their hats and gloves. Then she opened the front door to the theater.

"We'll be back," Mrs. Jansen told the woman who collected the tickets.

The snow had been cleared from the sidewalk in front of the theater. Beyond that there was only a narrow path. Eric walked behind Cam as she followed her mother to the Jansens' car. They worked together to clean the snow off the windows. Then, while Mrs. Jansen started the car, she asked Cam to please tell her who took the film.

"When I said all those *'Clicks,'* I was looking at the people I saw in the lobby. Angela Kane was there wearing a big red hat. When Dad saw her in line, he thought she was one of the actors in *Shoe Escape*. Well, she was."

"What does that mean?" Eric asked. "So what if she was in the movie? That doesn't mean she stole the film."

Cam's mother was holding the steering wheel firmly with both hands. She was driving very slowly through the falling snow.

"When you said all those *'Clicks,'* did you see something else?" Cam's mother asked.

"Yes. Angela Kane was just ahead of us when we bought the popcorn. She wanted change to use in the pay telephone."

"Do you think she's the one who called

the man in the projection booth?" Eric asked.

"Yes. That's just what I think," Cam said. "And when he came to the phone, no one was there because Angela Kane was on her way to the projection room to steal the film."

"This is Taft Drive," Mrs. Jansen said. "And there's a good spot to park. It's almost all clear of snow. Someone must have just pulled out.

"But why would she take the film? What was her motive?" Cam's mother asked as she parked the car.

"I don't know," Cam said.

"She's probably not even home," Eric said. "She's probably still at the theater watching *The Monster Spiders*."

Number 358 Taft Drive was an apartment building. The front door was open. Cam's mother looked at the mailboxes and found Angela Kane's name. She lived on the first floor.

When they reached the door of the apartment, Eric whispered, "I still think Mr. Bender took the film. He has a motive."

Mrs. Jansen knocked on the door. She waited. Then she knocked again, louder.

"Just a minute," a voice called from the other side of the door. "Who is it?"

"I'm Helen Jansen. I'm here with my daughter, Jennifer, and her friend Eric Shelton."

The door opened, but only a few inches. A chain lock kept the door from opening any wider.

"Are you Angela Kane, the actress?"

"Yes, I am."

"I've wanted to meet you for such a long time!"

"Oh, a fan, a fan," Angela Kane said as she unhooked the chain lock. She opened the door wide and said, "Come in. Come in. I'll show you my movie posters, and you'll probably want my autograph."

Mrs. Jansen walked in first. Cam and Eric followed her. The apartment was one room. There was a small kitchen, an unmade bed, a table, and a few chairs. The walls were decorated with movie posters. One was for *Shoe Escape*.

"I was in all these movies," Angela Kane said as she pointed to the posters.

She was a tall, thin woman, about the same age as Mrs. Jansen. She was wearing a long brown dress with a bright orange scarf as a belt and a great many necklaces and bracelets. When she pointed to the posters, the jewelry banged together and jangled.

"I had no idea you were in so many movies. You're a real movie star," Cam's mother said.

"Take a look at this one," Angela Kane said. She pointed to one of the posters.

While Cam's mother read each of the posters, Cam and Eric looked around the apartment. Then Eric pulled on Cam's sleeve and whispered, "Look on the bed."

Chapter Seven

Cam looked on the bed. Then she whispered to Eric, "It looks real sloppy, don't you think?"

"Look under the sheet," Eric whispered. A small part of a flat gray can was uncovered. "I'll bet that's the film."

Cam's mother and Angela Kane were standing in front of the *Shoe Escape* poster. Mrs. Jansen said, "My husband and I saw this movie just a few days before we were married. It's one of his favorites. It's a pity *Shoe Escape* isn't shown more often."

"I wasn't very good in that one," Angela Kane said softly.

"Yes, you were. It's such a good movie, and you were wonderful in it. We were just at the Hamilton Movie Theater. We went to see *Shoe Escape*, but something happened to the film."

Cam pulled on the sleeve of her mother's coat. She wanted to tell her about the flat gray can. But her mother kept talking to Angela Kane.

"I hope you don't mind if I sit down," Cam's mother said as she sat right next to the gray can.

Angela Kane quickly pulled at the bed sheets until the can was completely hidden.

"Is that the missing film?" Cam's mother asked.

Angela Kane nodded.

"Why did you take it?"

Angela Kane began to cry. She took a tissue from her pocket and wiped her eyes.

Cam and Eric looked at each other. Then they looked down at the floor. It seemed wrong to watch an adult cry.

"I was going to be a real star," Angela Kane said. "But that movie ruined me. That was the last acting job I had. I didn't intend to steal the film today. I just wanted to watch it. But when I got to the theater, something happened to me. I didn't want to see that movie. And I didn't want any one else to see it."

Cam's mother took the film from under the sheet and said, "You know, you'll have to return this."

"And just because you didn't get any more acting jobs doesn't mean that you weren't good in *Shoe Escape*," Cam said. "Maybe the movie people didn't know where to reach you."

"Or maybe they just didn't have the right parts for you," Eric said.

Angela Kane went back to the theater with Mrs. Jansen, Cam, and Eric. In the car she told them about her first movie role. "The director told me to look frightened, but I just couldn't. Then he took a toy mouse from his pocket. I was so scared. I was shaking. 'That's it!' the director yelled. 'Don't lose that look.' "

When they entered the theater, the police were in the lobby with the theater manager and Mr. Bender. They were arguing with Mr. Bender.

Cam ran up to the theater manager. "Here's the film," she said as she gave him the gray metal can. "Mr. Bender didn't take it."

Angela Kane told the theater manager what she had done. And she told him why.

49

Mrs. Jansen told him how Cam used her amazing memory to find Angela Kane and that Eric had noticed the missing film.

Mr. Bender took off his coat. "You owe me an apology," he said to the theater manager. "And you owe me my money back. I paid to see two movies, and I didn't see either of them."

"We'll have to take you to the police station," one of the officers said to Angela Kane.

Cam, Eric, and the others watched as the police led Angela Kane out of the theater. The theater manager took some money from his pocket and gave it to Mr. Bender. As Mr. Bender counted the money, he told Cam's mother, "You know, at my theater, you get to see a triple feature—three great movies for the price of one."

The theater manager smiled when he heard Mr. Bender talk about his triple feature. Then the theater manager said, "Now, why don't you all go inside and watch *Shoe Escape*? It's a great movie."

The theater manager ran up the stairs to the projection room. Cam and the others went into the theater.

The Monster Spiders was just ending. A parade of normal-size spiders was crawling out of an open box. On the side of the box was a changing list of the names of the director and the stars of the movie.

"You missed a good movie," Cam's father said. "Where were you?"

"Jennifer found the missing film," Cam's mother said. "Now we can see the next part of *Shoe Escape*."

People were beginning to leave the theater when the theater manager called to them from the stage. "Please don't leave. We'll be showing the rest of *Shoe Escape* in just a few minutes. But before it starts, I'd like to thank Jennifer Jansen, her mother, and Eric Shelton for helping us bring you this wonderful movie. And just a short while ago I made a terrible mistake. I'd like to apologize for that mistake to Mr. Dennis Bender, of Bender's Bargain Theater." The theater manager smiled and said, "It's the only theater in town with a triple feature— three great movies for the price of one."

People returned to their seats. The lights dimmed. Then the screen lit up with a picture of hundreds of shoes crowded inside an elevator car.

Chapter Eight

The elevator stopped in the lobby of the office building. When its doors opened, the shoes walked out to the street. Thousands of other shoes were already there. Cars stopped. Horns were honking. There was a huge traffic jam. People standing on the sidewalk just stood and watched as the shoes marched past.

"I wonder where they're all going," Cam whispered.

Helicopters with news reporters inside circled over the parade of shoes. While the newsmen were reporting what was happening below, the threads of their shoes opened up. The shoes came off their feet and floated down in tiny parachutes to join the parade.

"That's funny," Eric whispered. "This movie makes you think that shoes are like people."

"There must be millions of shoes," Cam said. "And look, there are sneakers, roller skates, slippers, and little baby booties marching, too."

As the shoes marched, they stopped traffic. They crushed flower gardens, kicked down trees and telephone poles.

They all marched to the gates of the mayor's house. One boot was carrying a large sign that said: "WE'RE TIRED OF BEING STEPPED ON AND STEPPED IN."

"This is the greatest march our town has ever seen," a television reporter said in front of a set of cameras. "Shoes from all over the world have come here."

"That reporter is Angela Kane," Cam said.

"The shoes want to see the mayor," the reporter said. "I hope he comes out soon."

Angela Kane reported about the mayor's schedule and the type of shoes he wore. She also described the many different shoes that marched to the mayor's house.

"The front doors of the house are open-

ing. The mayor is coming out," Angela said.

"Look," Eric said, "that's not the mayor coming out. It's a monster-size shoe."

The millions of shoes around the mayor's house gave out a loud cheer. Then the movie screen showed Angela Kane. She was still talking into the microphone. As she talked, the screen showed her feet. They were bare. The movie ended, and the lights in the theater went on.

"What does that mean?" Cam asked her father.

"The shoes have won. It means that people have to walk around in bare feet from now on."

"What will happen to Angela Kane at the police station?" Cam asked.

"I don't know. She might have to pay a fine. She might have to spend some time in jail."

The theater manager and Mr. Bender came over to where Cam, Eric, and Cam's parents were sitting. They were both smiling.

"We're friends now," the theater manager said.

"I like what he said about my theater," Mr. Bender told them. "But we both have a question about Jennifer's mental camera. Does it take still pictures or moving pictures?"

"Still pictures," Cam said. "I just look at something, say 'Click,' and a still picture is stored in my head."

The theater manager smiled and said, "Then if you want to see moving pictures, you'll have to come to one of our theaters. And for the next three months you can all come for free. Just tell the person at the ticket booth who you are."

"And don't forget," Mr. Bender said. "At Bender's Bargain Theater—"

Cam, Eric, Cam's parents, and the theater manager started to laugh. Then they all said, together with Mr. Bender, "You get to see a triple feature—three great movies for the price of one!"